# WHAT THE
# DINOSAURS
## DID LAST NIGHT

# WHAT THE DINOSAURS DID LAST NIGHT

REFE & SUSAN TUMA

LB
LITTLE, BROWN AND COMPANY
New York   Boston   London

Little, Brown and Company
Hachette Book Group
1290 Avenue of the Americas, New York, NY 10104
littlebrown.com

First Edition: October 2014

Little, Brown and Company is a division of Hachette Book Group, Inc.
The Little, Brown name and logo are trademarks of Hachette Book
Group, Inc.

The publisher is not responsible for websites (or their content) that
are not owned by the publisher.

The Hachette Speakers Bureau provides a wide range of authors for
speaking events. To find out more, go to hachettespeakersbureau.com
or call (866) 376-6591.

ISBN 978-0-316-29459-1
LCCN 2014940631

10 9 8 7 6 5 4 3 2 1

WOR

Design by Gary Tooth / Empire Design Studio

Printed in the United States of America

For Adeia, Alethea, Leif, and Amarie. Never stop playing.

It doesn't matter what it is. What matters is what it will become.
— **Dr. Seuss**

Everything you can imagine is real.
— **Pablo Picasso**

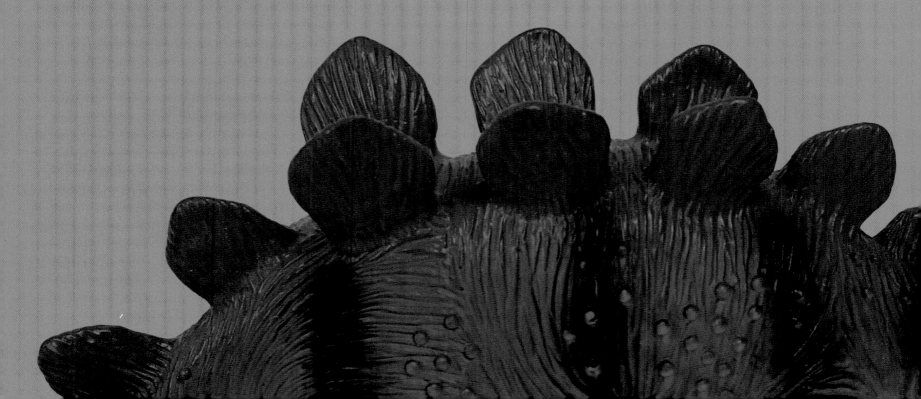

# WHAT THE
# DINOSAURS
## DID LAST NIGHT

# Introduction

**Every November night our house is vandalized** by a gang of plastic dinosaurs. It happens while the family sleeps. Dishes are shattered, food is spoiled, and walls are defaced by tiny case-molded claws. Nothing is safe. Our kids wake up each morning and burst into our room, exclaiming, "Come see what the dinosaurs did last night!" They pull Susan and me out of bed and drag us to the latest dinosaur scene. "Take a picture!" they say, knowing that, without evidence, no one would believe us.

For years our growing family lived peacefully, if a bit uneventfully, in a small house in suburban Kansas City. I worked a series of jobs that paid decent wages and provided varied levels of personal fulfillment. Susan worked, too, but after the birth of our second child, she transitioned into life as a full-time stay-at-home mom. As part of this new role, she took on creative endeavors wherever she could find them: oversized cardboard boxes became castles and pirate ships, rolls of tinfoil became robot antennae and shining armor. I would come home from work and transform into Blackbeard the pirate or a creature from outer space. Adeia and Alethea, then ages five and four, lived part-time in a makeshift fantasy world.

Part-time. Because, of course, there was "real life," too, and real life never wants for challenges. Raising two kids was hard work. Susan and I frequently felt outmatched and ill-equipped. We got stressed, we fought; sometimes we simply didn't have the energy to play.

Our son, Leif, was born in 2011. We loved him from the moment we laid eyes on him, and our adoration for that fiery little redhead only grew each day. But there were complications. He had health problems that, while far from life-threatening, meant sleep became an increasingly rare commodity. For his first two years, he woke up in pain three, often four times each night. We spent hours walking with him, singing to him, telling him stories. Susan and I had to learn to function on an average of four hours of sleep. Our days were spent in doctors' offices and on the phone with specialists. Parenting is always an around-the-clock job, but as the days and nights blurred together during those first years with Leif, we wondered if the clock was even working.

Sleeplessness quickly began to take its toll. Susan and I forgot things, misplaced keys and cell phones, and burned dinners. We lacked the patience to solve simple problems for our girls when they didn't want to share a toy or couldn't agree on a cartoon. We awoke most mornings more exhausted than when we went to bed the night before. It wasn't long before our two oldest noticed. Cardboard castles and space-ships were replaced with TV shows and iPad games, day trips to the zoo with day after day inside the house. It was hard to get down on our kids' level to play when we felt like we might not be able to get ourselves back up again. We needed a way to reconnect.

Toward the end of the summer of 2012 Susan's parents sent a truckful of hand-me-downs they were getting rid of in preparation for a move. We made off with a good haul: a few pieces of furniture, a grill, and several boxes of toys. Most of the toys belonged to Susan's younger sisters and were dolls and dress-up clothes that quickly disappeared into our daughters' room. But there was a single box from Susan's brother. It was full of superhero action figures, Star Wars toys, and a few plastic dinosaurs. The dinosaurs had seen better days. Their paint had been scratched away by countless adventures, and their plastic joints showed signs of cracking. More than one of the dinosaurs' tails had worn down to a nub at the tip. The girls didn't show much interest in their uncle's hand-me-downs, so we tossed them into an old toy box, already home to some Ninja Turtles and a few other dinosaurs from our own childhoods. We set the box aside, figuring we'd save it for our son when he was old enough. For months, the toy box was rarely opened.

The next time we saw those dinosaurs was on Halloween. It had been a difficult day. Leif's sleepless nights had gotten worse. Trick-or-treating had been canceled because Adeia was sick, and the kids had gone to bed disappointed and emotional. Susan and I were exhausted, cleaning up after another day spent cooped up inside the house. We could tell our daughters had been desperately bored because even the neglected contents of that toy box had been dumped all over the living room floor. Susan started sorting through them as she cleaned, and held up a couple of the dinosaur figures.

"I remember these," she said. "I always loved them."

As we got ready for bed, Susan set the dinosaurs on the bathroom sink where our daughters would find them the next morning. I asked what she was doing and she shrugged.

"Just having a little fun."

We went to bed without giving it another thought.

The next morning, our daughters nearly broke down the door to our room.

"Mom and Dad, you have to see this!" Alethea said. "The dinosaurs came to life last night—we caught them brushing their teeth!"

Susan and I dragged ourselves out of bed as the girls looked on impatiently. As soon as our feet touched the floorboards, they grabbed our hands and pulled us into the bathroom. At first glance, it seemed as if the dinosaurs were exactly the way Susan left them—standing in the same places, frozen in the same positions. Then, we looked closer. We looked at our girls' faces and saw the way they smiled and how their eyes had grown wide. We realized that, sure enough, the kids were right: the dinosaurs *had* come to life. And, with that, we knew they would do it again.

### DINOVEMBER

The mischief began modestly enough. After that first night in the sink, the dinosaurs climbed onto the kitchen table and tore open a box of cereal, spilling whole-grain squares all over the floor. Our girls were delighted and asked if they could still eat the cereal for breakfast.

"Do dinosaurs have germs?" they asked. The plastic ones don't, we assured them.

The next morning, we discovered the dinosaurs had made a mess of the fruit bowl, helping themselves to bananas, oranges, and strawberries. Even the carnivores got in on the action. After that, they breached the refrigerator door and found an unguarded carton of eggs—eggs that they promptly cracked all over the kitchen floor.

"Uh-oh," we heard the girls whisper. "Mom and Dad are not going to like this."

The dinosaurs proved to be less than tidy. They covered a dining room wall in crayon, leaving half-chewed wax all over the floor. They broke Susan's favorite vase, unraveled an entire package of toilet paper in the bathroom, and engaged in an ill-fated attempt at baking cookies. One night, they went so far as to build an elaborate zip line, stretching across the dining room ceiling from the French doors to the chandelier. Each morning was a new adventure.

"Do you think they'll come to life every night?" Adeia asked. She was showing us the "field journal" she had created to track the dinosaurs' activities. The pages were filled with drawings of the various messes in surprising detail, along with depictions of the individual dinosaurs. Susan and I looked at each other.

"Maybe they'll do it for the whole month," Susan said.

"Dinovember," I said, and Adeia ran off to find her sister and tell her the great news.

We took our first pictures of the dinosaurs about a week in. Our girls were telling anyone and everyone who would listen about their magical, misbehaving toys, and our friends and family were starting to ask questions. What exactly was going on at our house? Posting photos of the dinosaurs online allowed us to share Dinovember with the people we loved, and allowed those people to follow along and enjoy the adventure with us. Our kids felt like they had found a game that everyone could play with them, from their classmates at school to their aunts and uncles in Chicago and their grandparents in Hawaii.

It was the pictures that transformed Dinovember from something that was exclusively for our children into something that was fulfilling for us, too. It had been a long time since we'd had a means of expressing our own creativity. We didn't have the time, we didn't have the money, and God knows we didn't have the energy. In a way, getting down on the floor and shooting pictures of those dinosaurs brought Susan and me back to a time before we had kids and jobs and obligations, when the only future we could foresee was filled with creativity and possibility.

Then, on December 1, the kids woke up and searched the house, looking for what the dinosaurs might have gotten into the night before. But the house was clean. No spills, no destruction, no dinosaurs. Dinovember had come to an end.

"Do you think they're hibernating?" our daughters asked.

"Seems that way," we replied. "We'll have to wait and see what happens next year."

Over the following weeks, life got back to normal. The kids were disappointed that Dinovember was over—our friends and family, too. But we began to notice subtle changes around the house. The girls played more with their toys and stuffed animals. They invented elaborate stories and games, entertaining themselves for hours on end. They asked for TV time less frequently. Adeia had always been a thoughtful, articulate kid with an analytical mind and a thousand and one questions. After Dinovember, we could swear she seemed more comfortable with the unknown. Instead of relying on us to answer all her questions, we witnessed her imagining possibilities herself—from the practical to the fantastic—and forming her own hypotheses. The field journal she'd started for the dinosaurs expanded to include birds and insects, cloud formations ("That one's a bunny"), and observations about the weather. Were the dinosaurs responsible for these changes? Maybe. We'll never know for sure. But we like to think they played a part.

## BACK TO NORMAL

The year 2013 was a big one for the Tuma family. Alethea started preschool, and Leif was walking and talking and finally sleeping through the night. We welcomed another addition in October—Amarie, a beautiful baby girl. There were new challenges now. The kids outnumbered us two to one. Money and time were tight. We struggled to adjust to the dietary restrictions that alleviated the pain that had been keeping Leif awake at night. We saw much of our extended family move far away. November was just around the corner, and our world was a very different place from the year before.

"Will the dinosaurs come alive again?" Alethea asked. Susan and I looked at each other.

"I don't know," I said. "It might have been a onetime thing."

"I hope they do," Alethea said. "I miss them."

It wasn't the first time the kids had asked about the dinosaurs. Every few weeks, they would dump out the box and reenact scenes from Dinovember. They would come find us and tell us the dinosaurs had made another mess.

"But when will they do it for real?" they asked.

And it wasn't just our kids. We were getting calls from our friends and family, too.

"It's almost November," they said. "We can't wait to see what the dinosaurs get up to this year!"

Susan and I could only smile and shrug. We hadn't thought much about whether or not the dinosaurs would repeat their activities. It had been a wonderful experience, but we had a new baby and plenty of other things going on. Could we handle the dinosaurs' return?

## DINOVEMBER 2013

In the end, we were powerless against the coming invasion. It would mean more late nights, more hard work, and more broken dishes, but also an entire month of excitement for our kids. It was just too much fun to pass up. So, the dinosaurs returned—with a vengeance. They knocked over the kids' leftover Halloween candy and gorged themselves on Tootsie Rolls and lollipops. They mistook our houseplants for a jungle. They got into the girls' Barbie clothes and threw an uncharacteristically refined tea party. Nothing in the house was out of their reach.

The kids were thrilled that the dinosaurs' yearlong hibernation was over. The toys were up to their old tricks again, and every morning was like Christmas.

"Mom and Dad!" they would say, leaping into our bed. "Look what the dinosaurs did last night!"

Leif was in awe of the dinosaurs. He had been too young to understand or appreciate what happened the year before, but now he was the most enthusiastic of the bunch. Dinovember was a dream come true for him—dinosaurs, mischief, and destruction. And Mom and Dad didn't even get upset!

Adeia was more hesitant. She'd turned six that year, and though she still smiled and laughed at the dinosaurs' antics, we could tell she was processing the events, deciding what she thought about them. We heard her talking with her little sister when she thought we weren't around.

"Do you think they really come to life?" she said.

"Yes," Alethea said. "Don't you?"

"Of course I do," Adeia said, but she didn't sound convinced.

Once, she even went so far as to ask us if we were really behind the dinosaurs.

"What do *you* think?" I asked her. She didn't answer. We could see the wheels turning in her mind.

The next morning the kids awoke to the biggest mess the dinosaurs had ever made. Somehow, during the night, they had gotten into the garage and found a few bottles of spray paint. They had tagged the living room walls with black and yellow and pink, drawing cartoon dinosaurs and prehistoric slogans. The kids couldn't believe it. When they ran into our room that morning, even Adeia was speechless. As we stood in the living room, surveying the scene, she turned to her sister. "Now I'm sure they're alive," she announced, flashing us a knowing smile.

As the month went on, something strange happened—stranger even than usual. While we dealt with the dinosaurs in our own home, we began hearing reports of other families having similar experiences. Dinosaurs were making pasta in Italy, tending bar in New York, building Lego cities in Switzerland, and painting handlebar mustaches on the faces of sleeping children in London. Classrooms were invaded, along with libraries, museums, and restaurants. Dinosaurs were getting into trouble all across the world. Dinovember had become an epidemic.

Still, not two weeks later, the month of November came to an end, and with it ended the mischief of the dinosaurs. The toys went back into their boxes for some well-deserved rest, and the kids were left to wonder what might be in store for them next year.

IMAGINATION INVASION

At its heart, Dinovember is a celebration of imagination. Imagination is both a prerequisite for participation and, ultimately, what we hope to inspire. We want to train our kids to value their creativity, to cultivate imaginative thinking, and to look past what's possible.

It seems fitting that our guides throughout all of this should be dinosaurs. Nobody's ever met a dinosaur. They lived and died millions of years ago, long before the first histories were etched into cave walls. The once-mighty creatures now persist only in fossilized bones, tooth fragments, and impressions in rock. The men and women who study these fossils must come to their conclusions in the face of so many unknowns: What was the texture of their skin? What color were their eyes? How long did they live? Did they have feathers?

The questions we have about dinosaurs may never be definitively answered. Yet scientists use the evidence available to them to imagine the most likely possibilities and form hypotheses that go on to affect how the rest of us view the prehistoric world. Science is often viewed as exacting and noncreative, but without the well-honed imaginations of scientists and researchers, we would know precious little about the world around us.

Adeia, especially, seems to have taken this to heart. We asked what she wanted for her seventh birthday. A microscope, she said. She wanted to be a scientist. We were surprised at first. For the past few years, Adeia had spent most of her free time drawing. Crayons, colored pencils, and paints were her constant companions. She had told us many times that she wanted to be an artist when she grew up. When we asked about this, she told us, "I'll just do both."

And why not? Why can't our kids be painting paleontologists, singing accountants, or novel-writing programmers? Adeia may change her mind about her desired vocation a thousand more times before adulthood—and maybe well into it, if she's anything like me—but the fact that she sees art and science as compatible disciplines is a beautiful thing.

The dinosaurs have unwittingly taught Susan and me a similar lesson—that we can be parents and people at the same time. We've often felt like we had to be either the parents our kids needed or individuals with our own hopes and dreams— never both at once. When we tried in the past, we seemed to be maintaining two different identities, taking them on and off like costumes in a Metropolis phone booth. We've played with enough plastic dinosaurs by now to know that it doesn't have to be that way. Our kids aren't a hindrance to the things we want to do—they're integral to everything we do. They're our partners in crime and our grass-stained, runny-nosed muses. They're part of the story we're telling, and, one day, we'll be part of theirs.

Thankfully, the dinosaurs have shown no signs that they will follow their ancestors into extinction anytime soon. They will likely continue their high jinks as long as our kids are willing to believe. That could be many years for our youngest, Amarie, and as few as one or two for our oldest. Or maybe they won't outgrow it. Maybe they will always choose to believe and imagine the impossible. I can't think of anything more fun than that.

—Refe Tuma

The box said "well-balanced," but the dinosaurs were happy to prove it wrong.

Normally, carnivores don't eat *with* herbivores.
Then again, herbivores aren't normally made of plastic.

Climb up and get the plant, they said. It'll be easy, they said.

Whatever these are, they don't taste nearly as interesting as they smell.

When you're the last of your species, it's important to find
a creative outlet for all those pent-up feelings.

We're pretty sure dinosaurs aren't covered under our dental plan.

This seems like a harmless prank, until you remember that dinosaur feet have enormous, razor-sharp claws.

The dinosaurs invent a new game—Excavate the Paleontologist.

What kind of strange paradise is this, where eggs by the dozen are left unguarded in their nests?

This is just one of the many reasons dinosaurs don't wear clothes.

Spelunking takes a dangerous turn when the helpless duck
is nearly lost to a mysterious undertow.

The dinosaurs put their natural proficiency for scavenging to good use, coming up with nearly enough change for a stick-on tattoo.

The risk of melting plastic is nothing compared
to the glory of hot, crispy bacon.

Rex may never be the same again.

Getting him to fall for the trap was easy.
Getting it off proved more difficult.

Why hunt when you can stand in a bowl and let food tumble directly into your mouth?

This truly is a land flowing with Milk Duds and Bit-O-Honey.

Movie night hits a little close to home.

Either the dinosaurs have finally decided to pull their weight
around the house, or they've just discovered bubbles.

...or they simply wanted the dishes clean for when they smashed them.

"I told him it would be good for his spines."

The dinosaurs have learned that the human children will always lead them to the best food.

This is basically what it looks like when the kids use craft supplies, too.

"Look—I am a puny human. Take my picture!"

The dinosaurs really trash the place this time.

Ancient man bared his soul on the walls of his cave.
Plastic dinosaurs use refrigerator magnets.

Sadly, the zip line is not strong enough to hold the weight
of a full-grown human. How we know that isn't important.

Rex likes to take care of himself. You never know when you might meet
an attractive parasaurolophus or allosaurus with a thing for purple.

Tonight's screening explores prehistoric family dynamics and paternity issues.

The dinosaurs skip the discovery of fire and jump straight to electrical engineering.

The brachiosaurus is suddenly very conscious of the similarities
between his long yellow neck and what's for dinner.

"This is just like my uncle's place back home."

Many dinosaurs are believed to have been
fearless predators. That's mostly true.

Rex does his best to maintain his gruff exterior, but he's secretly
pleased with the way this dress flatters his delicate wrists.

The dinosaurs lose their Christmas spirit when they realize that St. Nick's been stiffing them for over one hundred million years.

Steggy faces a crisis of identity—root for the quadrupeds or his bipedal friends?

Medicine has come a long way since the days of lying sick in the mud, waiting for a larger predator to eat you.

For a species that still sleeps on the ground, the comforts of the modern world are a constant source of entertainment.

They couldn't believe that with all the tar pits back home,
they had never thought to try this before.

Dinosaurs are not easily housebroken.

In the old days, all it took to keep the romance alive
was a fresh troodon carcass and a cheeky roar.

Being encased in Jell-O is a lot like being fossilized,
except that you can eat your way out.

At least they didn't find the gin...

As they consider their culinary feat, the dinosaurs' sense of pride is quickly replaced with acute feelings of inadequacy.

The dinosaurs break out some old-school rock and roll. Like, really old-school.

Rex's killer layup proves that arm
span isn't everything.

The dinosaurs discover a portal to a vast new realm.

The modern world is full of strange and wonderful beasts.

We brought the dinosaurs back into the house, but it was too late—they'd already had a taste of the outside world.

It's not every day you dig up a dinosaur with his bones still on the inside.

If you're going to loot and pillage, it helps to dress appropriately.

The dinosaurs vow to one day find the fertile lands of Mallow,
where the marshfruit hang heavy on the vine.

For one fleeting moment, the dilophosaurus think they are
finally experiencing the phenomenon humans call "snow."

Perry finds his constant typecasting a bit hard to swallow.

The Order of the Plastic Fist.

"Reveal the source of your power, tortoise ninja!"

Is it a masterpiece or a mess? True art can't be put into a box like that.

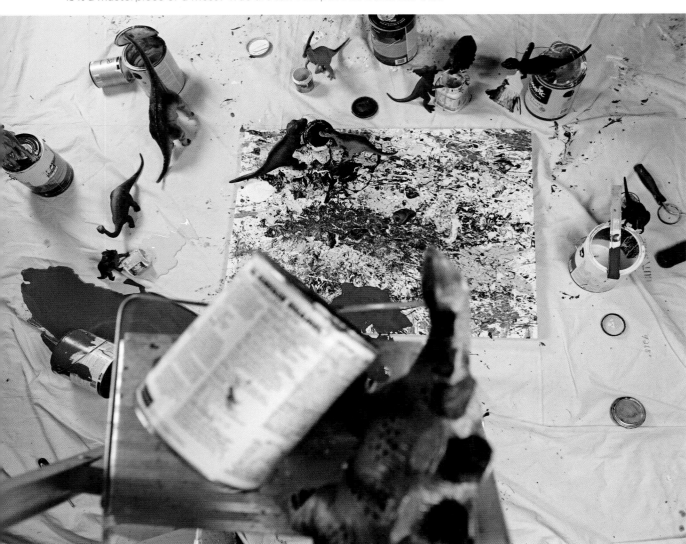

The dinosaurs help Steggy ring in his 150,000,000th birthday.

Even dinosaur toys can't resist playing with dinosaur toys.

"You said humans do this for fun?"

Polly tried to explain that birds and dinosaurs share a common lineage, like one big family. Unfortunately, there's just no reasoning with a hungry dinosaur.

If destroying our house is a superpower, we have yet to determine the dinosaurs' Kryptonite.

Meat slurry: the true carnivore's protein shake.

Even the proudest hunters can't say no to food delivered right to the front door.

Any hope of containment is dashed when the dinosaurs gain access to the air vents.

The dinosaurs attempt a dangerous technique developed by a
reclusive Geneva scientist to transform plastic into living tissue.

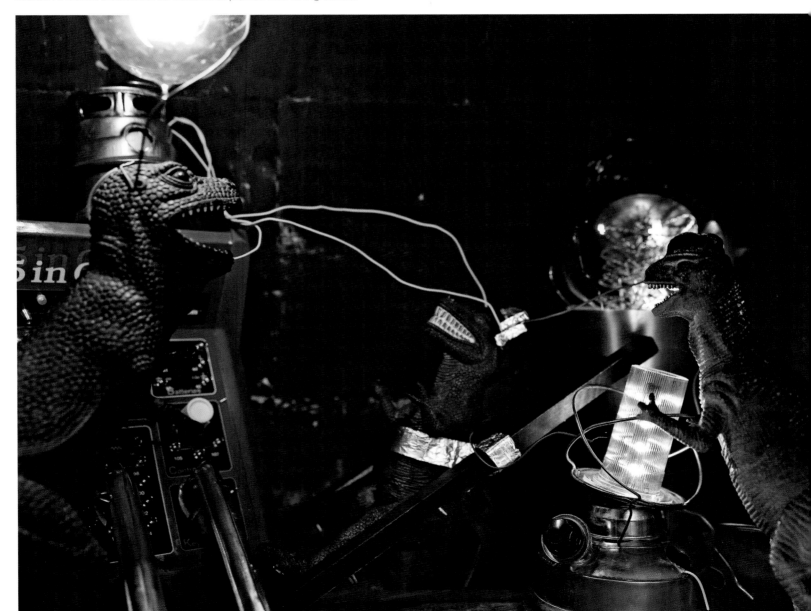

The dinosaurs turn to art therapy to help them come to terms with their own nature as sculpted plastic.

The dinosaurs haven't experienced a brain freeze like this since the Pleistocene glacial epoch.

Steggy practiced for weeks, knowing he may never have another chance to play the carnivore.

When dinosaurs mark their territory, they make sure not to leave any room for interpretation.

Once their dominance over the house has been established, the dinosaurs decide it's time to do some redecorating.

The dinosaurs accidentally find themselves in an ice age of their own design.

Somehow, in all the manufacturer's product meetings and focus groups, an avalanche-prevention feature never came up.

We are not fans of the dinosaurs' latest stunt.

Rex always dreamed of soaring through the heavens like a pterodactyl, feeling the wind in his teeth.

On their final night, the dinosaurs party like they're going extinct.

## ACKNOWLEDGMENTS

We didn't set out to write a book about toy dinosaurs. We didn't set out to do anything of significance, really. It is our kids who, since the day they entered our lives, have taken whatever good might be found in us, whatever noble intentions we might have, and transformed them through the prism of their innocence into something worthwhile. So, first and foremost, we thank them for being exactly who they are.

Completing a book of this scale under such a tight deadline took more than what we were able to do on our own. Thankfully, we had our friends, our families, and our church to encourage us, get excited with us, and have fun with our kids for us while we were busy playing with toys.

We've also had a true dream team of agents and editors to guide us and help us shape this book into what it has become. John, Malin, Kristyn, Liz—we know exactly how fortunate we are to have you all by our side.

A few others deserve special mention: Rick Tuma, for teaching us the value of our childhood toys; Michelene Reed, for her efforts in dinosaur recruitment; Scott Jolley, for jump-starting our camera rig; Menga, for inspiring a deep love of imagination; our parents, for their unfailing support; and Marissa Anderson, for making it possible to have our kids right there with us during the making of this book.

We'd also like to thank each and every person who has participated in Dinovember and allowed their homes to be overrun with dinosaurs. We hope your lives and the lives of your kids are always filled with wonder.

## ABOUT THE AUTHORS

Refe and Susan Tuma live in Kansas City with their four children and a herd of plastic dinosaurs. The Tumas began cataloging their dinosaurs' antics in 2012, igniting the imaginations of hundreds of thousands of children—young and old—across the world.